AF189074

Virtual affairs

a short novel by

Paul Riedel

www.paul-riedel.de

©Paul Riedel, Munich 2018

Printed in Germany

Cover: © Paul Riedel, Munich 2018

First German Edition 2016

First English Edition 2018

Herstellung und Verlag:

BoD - Books on Demand, Norderstedt

ISBN 978-3-7460-6161-0

Paul Riedel

Born on May 27, 1960, in the Brazilian city of Sao Paulo as Paulo Sergio Riedel.

He uses the name of his great-grandfather as the artist name. He finished a successful career in the IT and data banks industry 2010 and is fully devoted to his art and literature since then.

Between 2007 and 2011 he learned psychotherapy but decided not to work with it. Most of his know-how in this aided him in his interest about the human nature.

His native Portuguese brands his novels by its rich vocabulary, just as his interest for the ancient history also contributes in his style.

Foreword

The world is changing, and melancholy can cloud our senses.

Abstinence of emotion is an increasing problem in our society, which is also triggered by our unstoppable technology development. Our first impulse is to feel hungry for any sign of emotion and on the other side, distrust grows and block ours sense.

How should we shape our life in the future?

If we believe to encounter any sweetheart in dating portals, think that reaching to find the long-sought dearest, it will destroy the business basis of the operator. The rising supply of dissatisfied love seekers increases his business perspectives. This result in a trivialization of the seekers, who get tired of a senseless search.

Economic principles of supply and demand are invading our privacy and altering our character.

In this short story, see how good faith and naivety can destroy a person.

Can you intellectually resist the assimilation through greater powers or missed to be a victim of an invisible technological mind?

Virtual affairs

Silence predominates in the room, and the sun light was far from showing itself on this summer day. White walls held a lighter ceiling and below they were carried by a carpet with a depressingly grey.

Office tables were almost indiscriminately distributed in the room, agreeing to the recommendation of some modern interior designers. The four men in the room glanced uncertainly at the grey floor. No cell phone rang. A humming could barely be heard in the next room.

On the monitor on the back wall, the image froze after the pause button had been pressed. A scene seemed to be taken from witty American soap operas. An Asian woman, a reporter, and flashes of light from countless sources stroke them. The stench of burned coffee drifted through the room and under the coat of silence that prevailed there, the heavy aroma was even unpleasant than usual.

"I can't explain that." howled a quite massive red-haired man named Angus. He was just over forty years old but looked like sixty. His last hair had already said goodbye to his head three years ago. Only at the temples were some faithful specimens of his former mane left. His face was wrinkled and reddish. In this agonizing circumstance, and with his tearful voice, his appearance resembled a figure of any ancient Greek stage play. His sentence finished in a sardonic grimace and he crouched down in his antique leather armchair.

"Too late for crocodilian tears, you prick." Toshi's voice sounded slightly threatening. Toshi lives in Germany since he was eleven years old. Three years ago, he moved to Munich. His Japanese origins were barely recognizable, except for the sharp-edged eyes and menacing look of an angry samurai.

"I've never talked to any virtual person about my most private life." Angus looked around in the crowd and searched in his memories for something he might have missed.

"However, this reporter lady even recalls details of your … love practices as well as details from our brinkmanship." Toshi switched off the espresso machine and walked out of the room with the glass pot in the direction of the kitchen, where a standard coffee maker stood. He was slim and looked quite dainty for a consultant in his position, but his very determined gait revealed his assertiveness. He had been working in politics for almost fifteen years and had very competent connections with all parties and politicians.

"You will have to resign. No politician can still hold office after such a disgrace." Siegfried was usually called Siggy, and he was always a kind person, but no one could doubt on his professionalism. He was always confident in his performances and how many political advisors. He was astute to succeed when needed. Many reporters knew that to have a conflict with Siggy, could also mean being forgotten at the next press conference. Even worse, they could be invited to an impossible seat at the rear. The situation in which they had been brought by a revelation was fatal to all concerned. As a consultant, he could only escape from this affair by making formal arrangements for everything and look for a new job.

"You are not the first man, who doesn't keep his cock in his pants. Anyway, you are at least the first one to be photographed in Thailand having sex with three transvestites. Crowning it posting the photo on the Internet." Siggy could hardly suppress laughter when he looked at the static image in the television monitor.

The office was modest and offered only a few useful accessories on the tables, two solitary art prints on the wall had some similarity to Matisse. This was not a proper scenario for such a drama. Angus had been on vacation three years ago with a friend in Thailand, whose he never had met again. Both had quarrelled about decency and fun, so that Angus flew back three days later than planned. He felt his moral slip was acceptable for a men's vacation. Angus thought that this friend might occasionally have made copies of the photos from his camera. That was more than unlikely, because Angus always had the camera with him, he remembered.

Surely, Angus's wife had certainly never poke around in his stuff. Even if she did it, she was unable to open an email program. It would have been sheer coincidence if she had recognized something.

The frozen scene on screen had some discretionary strips over Angus's penis and the phallus of fifteen-year-old Naidong. Naidong was one of the three transvestites, who seemed to want to satisfy Angus from behind. Angus fulfilled the scene laughing and stretching his buttocks, like an exposed pot-bellied faun, towards to Naidong.

Some could imagine the word 'ludicrous' in peculiar shapes, when watching this screenshot. Not a contribution for the afternoon movies program. Surely a picture that would reach the cover of all the muckraking newspaper of the city in the next day if they together don't react wisely and quickly. This was very evident to Angus.

Angus himself admitted that the picture may be a bit too rough for the conventional sense. During his vacation, he thought it was just hilarious. Now, a day before the announcement of an important bill, this mistake seemed no longer so funny to him at all.

The incident had really happened under disastrous circumstances, as it mostly occurs with late-puberty men on vacation. Angus and some friend tottered drunkenly through the unchaste streets of Koh Samui. Suddenly, both gentlemen were approached by three gorgeous *ladies*. As mostly usual in holiday resorts in Thailand, the ladies were invited to their hotel room. With champagne and beer, they undressed all their clothes unbridled. The photo was taken when they discovered that those three gorgeous 'ladies' were transvestites and really not women...based on the naked evidence of course. Angus found the mistake funny and so he decided to pose for this tragic photo.

Neither a psychologist, nor psychiatrist will ever understand what some men feel in such moments and even themselves would never be able to explain the situation. A mixture of shame, naivety and an excess of alcohol was an embarrassing mark in the lives of many people. Unfortunately, also in the disastrous Angus's life.

"And you are sure that nobody has seen this ... photo on the Internet?" Toshi has stormed into the room again with the clean-rinsed coffee pot. The break before the word *photo* gave a clear indication of his feelings, which mostly remained hidden.

The broadcast on-screen continued, and an eighteen-year-old Thai lady-boy told how the German Angus has loved him and paid for his trip to Germany and that he wanted to marry him very soon. Sure, the drag would never get an Oscar for this performance.

"He's lying!" Angus howled again and there was no doubt about the authenticity of his tears. He pondered and searched for words trying to make clear that he wasn't homosexual, what was absolutely irrelevant for his colleagues in this crucial moment. Angus's eyes ran red and swelled. This wasn't the first time in his political career, that the unexpected happened, but this occasion a solution seemed to exceed the capabilities of his assessors.

The broadcast came to its end with a smiling reporter wearing an atrocious red wig calling 'Back to the Studio!', followed by a subsequent heart-breaking Yowls from Angus, which filled the room.

In the next room arrived the first employee in the reception. She seemed not to have noticed the breaking news that arrived to all by E-mail last night.

"Angus, I think I've found something on your computer." Marcus, who had not said a word till this moment, silenced everyone. All three of them moved to the computer's monitor and saw a chat log that showed the photo from some Jemina67 sending back a kiss emoticon.

Marcus was the oldest in the group and a so-called faithful soul. He kept more secrets of Bavarian politics to himself than one even could imagine. He has been serving various politicians and even high-ranking military officials for over forty years. He was there since this office was established, cleaning up all rumours, photos and unpleasant comments about his supervisors from the social network. Social media reports, commentaries or photomontages... His careful eyes, which were currently supported by glasses, kept his opponents always in view avoiding all possible attacks.

"Marcus, how could you overlook that?" Siggy, who was a spokesman and always best dressed in this team, tried to understand the chronology of this incident.

"Our biggest enemy is Angus's dark side. If he trusted me his secrets, I would be able to take care of all the embarrassments in time. But he kept many details to himself." Yes, Marcus really hissed these words through his closed teeth. He was a little upset, because he would never allow himself such a mistake.

"Who is Jemina67?"

Disappointment is usually only a short time condition that vanishes as quick as it came. Marcus seemed to switch to professionalism and kept clicking on his keyboard. The glance of emotions he had, seemed to disappear from his face as quick as a short comb over his hair with his hand.

„Speak now!! ...and I don't want to hear fairy tales ..."

Toshi brought a little more emotion when demanding Angus to tell the truth.

"I think …" The adolescent girl from the reception brought a fresh pot of coffee and grasped the old one with her. She turned on the air-conditioning in the room, which the men obviously did not know. The air refreshed slowly, and as slow came words from Angus.

"Yes, she is a girl from Idaho, with whom I chat mostly once a week."

"Where and when?" Marcus kept clicking on his keyboard.

"This was really insignificant, she is just some woman from a website." Angus's appeasement wasn't successful.

"I advised you to do all your computer activities in this laptop and just in your apartment, but the log shows only part of a chat at My-Porn-Lady.info." Marcus rolled his eyes up to the ceiling and clapped his hands to his knees. "You deleted this chat and missed to tell me. You may use such pages, but not with your own name."

"I didn't use it. I'm called 'Thorshammer'. A pseudonym. No one knows me in Idaho and I have never boasted my name."

"The photo wasn't uploaded here in this station and I check your house connection daily."

"That was presumably the weekend I was with my sister in Oberammergau. I was bored and wanted to have some fun with Jemina. Something that every man does."

"No Angus, not every man and actually, we just want you to call your sister. Right now! Ask her to click on a link in the email, which I send and then leave the room. Ok? Got that?"

Angus nodded in agreement and moved to the phone. He shuffled instead of walking, apparently the adrenaline in his body made his legs stiff.

"Everybody knows that Angus is not a cultivate person. If he named himself Thorshammer, he should properly call himself Mjolnir, that would be at least the fitting name of Thor's Hammer." Although Toshi's comment was casual, it clearly indicated how little he appreciated Angus's behaviour and person.

"Just with a picture is impossible to locate some specific Thai drag or even guess Angus's name, I'm sure. He is not a renewed international politician and his meaning is still moderate." Siggy brought some the pieces of this uncommon puzzle together. He turned to his computer and brought the desktop to the projector on the wall. He drew a sticker with the photo in the middle of the chart and connected this icon with another symbol, representing Jemina67.

"I logged in the computer of Angus's sister. Angus deleted his log after the chat, but not completely. I can undelete some files."

Marcus clicked on an icon on his computer and there was the picture again.

"How do you do that?" Angus tried with low effort to turn the attention of the group from the subject and bring all to the wonders of the world of technology, which Marcus demonstrated. The photo disappeared in a deletion program and an old-fashioned noise of a paper-shredding machine was heard.

"Lamentably, I can rebuild part of the conversation because the streaming program only saves the last five minutes of the chat."

A video started, and Jemina appeared in a new personification of the naked Venus in a cheap bedroom. Half as elegant as the real Venus, Jemina presented herself in a hotel room with a lot of red velvet. The aroma of fungus under the shabby fabric could be smelled even in a virtual distance. While she lifted their legs along a pole bar to the beat of a techno version of a pop classic, she spoke with a hard accent.

She demanded that Angus come to the end. Angus whirled on the guest bed of his sister naked and waved around its thickish hands under his huge belly. Marcus suppressed his disgust - he had a lot of experience on that after so many years in this job.

Suddenly he played back and heard once more what she said: "Am I more attractive than your Thais?"

Angus moaned like a dying man in a horror movie. She said goodbye and the small picture of Angus blended to the full screen.

"Turn off the bullshit, please." Toshi tried to reduce his stress by rubbing his left thumb and forefinger over his eyes.

"Angus started a chat, but most of it was video chat. The conversation lasted thirty-seven minutes and I assume it was paid with ten tokens - with your personal credit card. You have declared it as play money. This, by all means Angus, can't really be true."

Marcus pointed to a scanned document on the monitor where value, transaction date and time could be clearly seen.

"Yes, but this credit card has no real account and you cannot associate it with me." Angus intervened.

"Toshi. I'm preparing a media coverage, in case that photo and press really come up to the news. I ask you, to find the source of this show with Marcus."

"Jemina67 already deleted her profile from My-Porn-Lady. But I've also noticed that the video shows another woman, who appears to be named Spitfire and who had a show on the internet about ten years ago. What means, our Angus saw was just a repetition. Dude, buy yourself a porn next time!"

"Do your job! I don't need to be humiliated. I'm still the environment minister."

Everyone turned back to their computer, ignoring Angus, who was urging for attention and seeking help to find a way out of the situation.

"How did you get notice of this website?" Marcus switched from Angus's sister's computer to his private laptop and logged into some of his various social media accounts.

"Oh, that was a tip from a buddy from a men's portal I've chatted, over two years ago. He has nothing to do with it. He once confided me that he visited this portal in some lonely hours."

"You logged in with your fake profile or did you make the mistake of connecting to the private one as well?"

"No. No way."

In fact, Marcus found out that Angus had kept to his instructions.

"Who and where happened such buddy contact?"

Marcus typed the address Angus had written on a note into the navigation bar of his browser.

"Another deleted profile. However, I have an idea about this. I think Jemina67 was the same person, who gave you the ... secret ... tip." As Marcus turned to face Angus, the lights of the ceiling reflected on his thick glasses. On this moment Angus got the feeling, that Marcus wasn't real.

The morning went quiet, and the four men prepared themselves for a fight: a press conference, press releases were sent and appointments with some supporters were made.

Anne dispatched all the other employees at the door and got them a day off.

The scandal was still under control.

Just before noon they came together again, and Marcus presented his results.

"I came with my research till four years ago and as it seems so far, that Angus has been here in contact with many virtual persons. With those he sometimes exchanged some gossip about our political plans. For few of those contacts he used his political account. I have managed those so far, and everything seemed to be fixed. Most of those unidentified contacts has been classified and the critical statements were reviewed by Toshi.

But Angus didn't keep us informed about his private life as agreed. Angus, we have always said that there should be no secrets between us."

Marcus showed his disappointment in Angus's behaviour.

"I compiled the findings from Marcus in my chart."

Siggy switched on the projector and a colourful picture appeared.

"It's clear Jemina67 never existed."

Angus crouched down and snorted.

It also becomes clear based on Jemina67's IP address, that she didn't come from Idaho and apparently her profile belongs to the same person who Angus contacted once, with one of his private fake profiles. And that's how Angus got in touch with an advertisement. This ad was a trap, addressed to his email account, so he thought it was a simple advertisement for dating portals. But Marcus is convinced that Angus has been observed with many different fake profiles for four years. All profiles on this chart have been deleted in the last twenty-four hours."

"With each of these virtual persons, Angus inadvertently discussed a small part of our environmental plans. We thought those statements have no repercussion, because we used them as a mood barometer in the social media. We wanted to know how the voters would react to certain statements."

Siggy was sweating despite the running air conditioner.

"Did we underestimate the danger of social media?" suggested Toshi casually.

"I think, sometimes yes."

After a keen glance in Angus's direction, Siggy adjusted his jacket and continued his explanation.

"Marcus has also find out that the statements informed to all these virtual persons were not many but combined were critical statements about our new environmental policy. It also looks like the person or group behind it wanted to know if Angus is an opponent of chemistry or not. Or maybe his attitude to antibiotics in pig farming. We never thought about this kind of evaluation of Angus's activities on the internet.

I have to say that we were not prepared for such a creative strategy."

"I'm still here." Angus objected.

"Did you hide any other phone-sex stories or other such inconveniences? Please Angus, do not make our life more difficult for us. Tell us all, before we have any more undesired surprises."

Siggy was not slim, but the large curves on his body were well placed as if he was a big cuddly bear. His blond hair was cut short, with an elegant hair parting to the left, where his smooth hair rested. Even if he acted to be threatening, he could not hide his charisma.

"Siggy, I don't do anything in life. I live from the office back to the home and from home back here. In the remaining time that my wife left for me, I need relax somehow. We don't have sex for five years. That drives any man mad."

Angus looked around and saw the questioning faces of his colleagues.

"I'm not gay." His voice was strident. He could not hold back his tears, and he covered his face with both hands.

"It was just for fun, man's amusement. Nothing else. We felt for drag queens and I thought it was funny and that's why we took those pictures."

"Pictures." Toshi stood up from the chair and whirled his arms in the air.

"I never posted anything in the social media or even showed anyone. Guys, what's up? It was harmless than a bachelor party."

"But the consequences for you are clear aren't they Angus? Or do you want to discuss this yourself with the press?" Siggy spoke chillier than usual, but Angus understood that everyone in the office after six hours of intense researches without a break were tired.

Angus shook his head and resigned. Just the thought of what he would experience with his wife when the scandal comes up, brought him to be silent.

"I have negotiated with the contact person from the news agency. They agree to forget this event with Nandong, the slut from Thailand, but they get exclusive coverage about the resignation from Angus." Toshi was rarely funny, but Angus interpreted his statement as fun.

"Naidong, not Nandong." Angus objected.

Toshi left the room for a moment and spoke in the front desk with the assistant.

"When I mentioned the resignation for personal reasons, they were very interested. Markus, can you scan his computers for photos?"

"Toshi. I can do everything if I know what I'm looking for. He certainly had this photo on his USB stick. I certainly cannot get in there over the Internet or Wi-Fi, but believe me … I checked his phone, tablet and even his various Virtual Drives. Everything I could reach is clean."

"I had already prepared his resignation speech, and I adapted it to some current circumstances. We have to discuss the performance with him."

"I clarify this with the party leadership, and will suggest Mrs. Richter as an interim replacement. So far, she has seemed to be scandal free and she would be the right front person for our campaign." Said Toshi.

"Mrs. Richter? She becomes my successor? What comes next?" Angus came back into the room and noticed the name of his opponent and realised that his career end in politics was now inevitable.

"Angus please, she's been working with us for years and she is quite popular. We need a quick solution and avoid a scandal. Do you have a better suggestion?"

"No. You're right. But if I imagine that she was once my assistant and now she'll be my successor, I feel really defeated."

The sun was barely exposed through the evening clouds. Air-conditioned rooms suffer on this unnatural effect. No matter what the weather outside look alike, you always have the feeling it's neither cold nor warm, but never like out there. They came in the conference room just before six and were exhausted.

A supplier entered the next room and got his money from the assistant.

You could see through the glass, as she went to the kitchen with two trays of sandwiches. She had initially refused to take coffee or other logistics services, but she developed well in her duties and understood that sometimes work had to be done with pride. This was unfortunately one of the times of crisis everyone had to lend a hand.

"I had something to eat because I thought it might save us some time." Angus tried to make his contribution with this gesture. Everyone thanked and went to the kitchen.

The mood was correspondingly at dinner. No jokes were heard like usual, no private topics, they ate and pondered. Even Anne, the assistant, did not sit there. She went out for a second and said she would come back at one.

"Toshi spoke to the party leadership. We will only mention disagreements as the reason for your resignation. The official version is you don't approve of the use of chemicals in pig farming and you consider it more honest to resign. This gives you the opportunity to get a good arrangement, your pension for example. Toshi asked them to allow you to keep the house staff for five years. This should be a good deal for you and no one takes damage. We will endeavour to place you in a charity organization that will only change your political career but not end it."

Siggy continued crunching on a thick baguette and the sound of crushed bread between his jaws reminded Angus of the Louis XIV's scaffold.

"I asked the reporter to make an offer to the Thai-boy and to get rid of him." Toshi saw the confused looks that focused on him.

"He'll no longer fly today and stays in Thailand with a large sum from our donation fund." All nodded in agreement and calmed down. Everyone knew donation fund was another word for bribes. They had five million there, which would certainly be enough to cover the damages of this situation.

"But you have to delete all photos and notes. Marcus and Angus, if there's any copy of some men's vacation anywhere, we'll have nothing to do with it in fifteen days. Is it clear to you?"

Toshi had been recommended to him because he was competent, neutral and a good advisor, always invisible. Despite all the problems, his name was never associated with his activities. Angus also understood that this was a kind of farewell and he knew nothing could go wrong with Toshi at his side.

"You can bet your life on it: I will never visit a chat room again."

"Porn videos cost only five euros, and everything is fine, nobody registers your data if you pay cash." Marcus poured himself a cup of tea and went back to his computer.

"The press conference is scheduled to take place at five o'clock. Do you feel ready for it?" Siggy worried more about his performance than Angus, realizing that his appearance was also his application for a new job.

The telephone in the central office rang. The sound of an ascending UFO was accompanied by a blue light, so that if the office was unoccupied, the call could be seen from outside.

The assistant wasn't there and so Marcus answered the phone. After a short conversation and a friendly smile, he called:

"Your wife, Angus." Then he added very softly with his hand over the mouthpiece: "She will not know about this scandal, and you don't have to talk about it." An old-fashioned wink showed that Marcus really belonged to an earlier generation.

Toshi talked to someone on the phone in the office and nodded several times. This seemed to clarify that he had understood everything was spoken. Perhaps a tradition, or culturally influenced, Toshi was always faithful and showed that was understood as was told.

Angus went to the phone and began to feel relief. He wanted to become a prominent politician in these years but noticed with disappointment that in politics there are no friends. Betrayal was rare to experience, but ready-made opinions and superficial disputes with other targets shaped handles in his party. Many gladly talked about the economic benefits for voters. Based on what he grasped in the past twelve years, that none of the decisions could make, had ever conveyed anything to the people. All decisions were linked to higher taxes or companies interest.

His colleagues were always superficially friendly and when met. They presented themselves with nicknames and hugged each other as if they were friends. Nevertheless, his appeals rarely were answered in less than three weeks by E-mail and greeting on birthdays or holidays never came without a request to comply with shortly afterwards.

Yes, it was a class of its own. His wife might overlook his slip-up after two days of anger and some revenge, but politicians would never forget that or even apologize.

He hung up the phone and no longer remembered what they uttered. He just knew she considered the anger in the air.

He walked slightly crouched with shame and was anxious about the upcoming press conference. He already had experience and the most unpleasant questions were assumed by Siggy. Siggy, known for some reporter house prohibition. His hardness was already well-known and that's why the reporters were always satisfied with his answers, even if it meant they did not mean anything.

The sky outside darkened, and one could just appreciate how cars drove by. People moved like in a silent movie, without sound.

"Angus, I've updated the chart by Siggy on the Board. I think you have carried yourself despite all caution to some discussions and thereby betrayed your intentions to the antibiotics policy to dishonest people." Marcus pushed his computer glasses up on his nose and pointed to the picture on the board.

"What do you mean?"

"In this professional portal, people must use their own names and false profiles are hardly possible. Personal recommendations and confirmations of ability or vita facts guarantee the authenticity of the profiles.

See the lady at the blackboard for instance."

Marcus made clears his example on the screen with a wave of his hand.

"She is a consultant at Pharmacom. Pharmacom is one of the antibiotic producers, who have the most to lose, if your bill is accepted. I was just considering why someone wanted to get background information from you using so many profiles and elaborated strategies."

Marcus stood up and demonstrated the connections between the distinct profiles and their relationships in the various social networks, until Jemina67.

"You can see someone has invested every possible effort to blame you. In Catholic Bavaria and in a time where morale in many areas plays a critical role, it became your Achilles heel. This was explicitly in your case.

I don't want to sound unfeeling, but nobody is a better victim for this strategy than you. Many know how you like to bluster, and proofs are not needed, one can easily assume some dark story in the background."

Toshi came into the room and listened to the speech.

The Assistant put her bag in the closet in the lobby and made ready to start the afternoon work.

"I'm sure that this picture is already circulating in some scandal groups and at the first questions from reporters will fatally come up. To neutralize you as a politician and make sure that you obtain an adequate supply, we should do as suggested by Toshi, I'm confident this will be the most efficient solution for all" Siggi briefly assumed the speech.

Marcus continued: "Anne will distribute some copies of this photo on the Internet. No excitement, please."

Marcus waved his hands like palm trees on the beach and explained:

"We can claim the original is just a photomontage. Placing montages photos in all the ridiculous blogs and tabloid press and declare this as an attack on the morale of the ministers. Without the Thai, no one can longer examine the authenticity of the photo and we urge your friend for discretion. To spread any wicked gossip about the topic will be easy."

Angus immediately interjected: "This won't be necessary. He himself will not want to be associated with this event anyway."

"Now, no matter how we get clean out of this scandal. You just have to do your part, but you're very persuasive in this subject, we all know that."

With these closing words, brought Marcus with his extensive experience the team to feel better and safe.

✦

The next following two hours Siggy wrote messages and invitations for an informal reception. There will be announced the Minister resignation for private reasons. Toshi took care of the last minutes management inviting colleagues of the faction and the competitors from other parties. All of them would be certainly having a interest in the vacant post.

"We must leave to our press conference." Siggi had new clothes for the event and didn't missed to visit the hairdresser. His appearance was always spotless and some even claimed to be enthralled by his performance, that they cared little about the content of his statements.

"I should make me fresh something prior the conference, isn't it?"

"We'll drive past you before. Marcus is informed and Siggi too, we can go then, or?"

"Guys, I will never forget this day and I thank you with my apologies for any inconvenience. For today, I want to say goodbye and ask you to let everything disappear as possible, and I again apologize for this infantile slip up."

"We are all grown up and definitely not squeamish. You should better have trusted us. We have avoided a more dramatic incident." Toshi sounded very upset and was too sensitive to recount the details of the raising scandal.

"Toshi. I never asked whether you're married."

"This should not be your business. Such details are not part of our relationship. I see." Cool and professional. Toshi knew the meaning of those words, and his skilful handling of statements was also his best skill as a keeper of so many secrets.

"Anyway, thank you also for your families, in case I generated them some stress."

Siggy and Angus were in the hallway and since there was no wall to the reception room, both gentlemen could be seen standing there.

A little bell announced the arriving of the elevator and the gentlemen said goodbye. Anne continued to flail uninterestedly at her telephone system.

"This was the fourth time we had averted such a scandal from Angus," Marcus smiled, slightly pleased.

"Unfortunately, we couldn't maintain him in this function any longer. Too many years in politics have the same effect as a degenerative disease." Toshi grabbed a cup of coffee and went to the phone. After a few minutes of phoning he came to the office and signalled Anne to switch on the press conference.

A camera pulled a close-up at Siggy's face and then zoomed back until almost his entire body was on focus.

"Right now, Environment Minister Angus Voigt will speak live to the Bavarian citizens. Obviously, the discrepancies among the minister and his party have escalated in one point of disruption between both, so he will explain his position. Some even said he offered to resign."

The commentator pretended to better know about some no existing backgrounds and tried his luck with guessing games. The reporter seemed to be quite acceptable in his forecast, but not good enough to know what was coming up.

"Dr Siegfried Rochner is always the first person in press conferences and he check microphones and…", a dramatic pause followed, "… if the press people are sitting accordingly."

Laughter followed, that seemed to have some special meaning for some viewers.

"Ladies and gentlemen, the responsibility of our Environment Minister lies on both: the environment and ethics, so that he represents the voters how expected. In the last months, he bravely fought against companies interests and did the pleasantest with ethical reviewed arguments. Jobs and tax revenues will be in danger, if the planned bans on antibiotics in pig farming are implemented."

A short protest in the rear of the viewers was weak to hear. Siggy was unimpressed and gave a short sign with an ambiguous look to one of the security persons of his staff. While the troublemaker was politely accompanied to the foyer, Siggy continued.

"Under these circumstances, our minister had to decide what is the best for the people and over his owns ideals. Thus, he felt cleverer to resign from his post at the end of the month."

"Ohs" and "Ahs" confirmed surprises in the crowd.

"Our Minister will answer your questions and if some can't be answered now, I assure you that we will send you a statement via email."

Minister Angus Voigt was waiting for the already prepared viewer's questions. Which somebody from staff would present on the microphone.

Everything went according to the plan and after five ready-made answers, which didn't necessarily fit perfectly to the asked questions, Siggy thanked the press and announced that invitations to the minister's farewell gala and the nomination of his successor would be sent soon.

All reporters asked almost at the same time as a chorus, who would be his successor, and as usual, Siggy waved very charming, which means who asks too much will not be invited to the coming gala.

Anne turned off the monitor, just before the program faded out.

"I think we did a good job. Greet your wife, Toshi."

"Sure. She comes back on weekend. She is profoundly impressed from Bangkok and wants to explore the city a little. Everything ran as expected. Now we can prepare us for our next job." Toshi confirmed.

"Isabella Richter has been flawless so far, and it almost sounds like she's coming from a monastery." Anne said.

"Voters will like to see that. A new Mother Teresa with many interest in environmental issues." Toshi said, somehow lost in his thoughts.

"Unfortunately, every saint has a stain under his cloak." Marcus knew that no one could resist the lure of internet.

"It's your problem to find any spot." Toshi augmented and laughed.

"I know your preferences very well and selected some conventions, where you will have marvellous recreational opportunities in addition to qualified contact. I'm sure you'll enjoy that rest."

Anne was friendly and well informed about the interests of her superiors. Her relationship with Marcus never made an issue, but she was as efficient as her grandfather.

"I'm sure you will be a good environment minister." Anne said with a friendly tone.

"And you will definitely be my best assistant. Thank you for the call."

Isabella Richter put the phone aside and felt like floating on clouds. She, who had previously held one deputy post, suddenly becomes a minister. Another woman at the top. That was not new in Germany, but at least it was her achievement and strength that brought her there.

She had to deal with the party program and get to know her team. She knew all of them and was sure they could do the job well. These guys were easy to coordinate.

Anne was almost inconspicuous, and her age could not be estimated. Instead of explaining the scars on her arm, she had always changed the subject cleverly. Siggy needed money for new designer suits and important press conferences. Marcus lived in the background. She preferred to talk to person of her own age than with older ones. Mostly she never understood the motivation or preferences from young people.

She disliked the idea to dictate letters. She probably could type the letter faster than most secretaries she knows. Anyway, her new career has new rules which she will learn. She had never been interested in computers and as a biologist, this wasn't to necessary at all.

As Anne told her on the phone call, the team will wait for first instructions and an informal talk at nine the next morning. She worried about Toshi because he was more dominant than the others. However, she knew if he causes problems, she could replace him at any time.

She was very experienced and had always been convinced to know the party program better than Angus did. She opened her closet and inspected the colours his clothes, considering what would be best for an informal get-together.

She saw a yellow dress that she had bought in Tunisia on her last vacation. The seller tried very hard to please her and sell his products, so that he evens accompanied to her hotel.

She felt a little uncomfortable because she didn't want to be confused with a sex tourist, but she did not want to miss the fun either.

She liked flying to countries like Tunisia, Morocco or Egypt. Excavations, beaches, many museums. Sometimes she visited interesting biology congresses that had much more closeness to nature than in Europe.

She chose a dark purple and arranged it on the hallstand. Matching shoes that didn't hurt.

She always wanted to be as elegant as the other office girls, but she couldn't. She couldn't walk on high-heels and her unfeminine stature that she inherited from her father, wasn't any help at all.

She reluctantly glanced in the mirror.

It was a career jump, but she wanted more.

Her husband had fled fifteen years ago and since then, she had only her career on focus.

When she realized she was already tired, she sat down at her desk and turned on the computer.

Besides the jazz that came from the radio, she heard the computer fan. As the system booted, she poured herself a Spanish cognac.

The system came up with many delay and she thought of Marcus and his first job to get her a new laptop.

She opened her browser and wrote "Tunisia" in the search field. Instantaneously interesting entries and news were listed. She read about a congress concerning environmental issues that will take place in Tunis in a few days and clicked on it.

She read the information and prices and was already too tired to navigate further, but an advertisement was still flashing on her eyes: a personal travel companion, who also speaks German and take care of all needs and could easily be reached in a new contact portal.

When the portal opened, there were several portraits of very good-looking men publicizing their experience in some form of a curriculum vita.

Clicking on the photo, were more pictures to see, even in swimming trunks.

She was fascinated with this new experience. She never saw anything like that in Tunisia before.

She was sure that no offer from Anne could better satisfy her expectations. A button below showed: "Chat with me."

When she pressed the button, a message came up: "I am Affar72. What is your name?"

After Remark

This is not my first publication in English, but my first short novel.

In case you have any suggestions about the text, I would be overjoyed to read your e-mail.

You can contact me in my web-site.

In 2018 I'm concluding forty years of artistical career and I hope soon to publish new title in English.

I already have sixteen books in German, and now my first in English.